HEARTS

ON

Fire

A 'FIREY' NOVELETTE

T0359161

Dragonfly Publishing

JENNY LYNCH

Copyright

A catalogue record for this work is available from the National Library of Australia

ISBN(sc): 978-0-6454370-0-3

ISBN (e): 978-0-6454370-1-0

Dedication

This book is dedicated to my number one fan, my mother, Barbara Walton, whose proofreading skills are second to none and who may or may not have been the inspiration behind the character of Lizzie.

Erin twisted and turned in front of the mirror, screwing her nose up at the red bodycon dress that hugged her curves—perhaps a little too well. Staring at the pile of discarded clothes on the floor, she winced, knowing she was out of options. Why did all of her clothes feel so snug? Surely it wasn't time to go up a size? A shopping trip after her next payday was definitely on the cards. But for now, this one would simply have to do. Perhaps she should have asked Amelie what the current dress code for a Hen's Night is.

Images of Amelie flashed through her mind— the older sister who had her life mapped out to perfection—with her gorgeous boyfriend and hair salon business partner Anton by her side, her own home, a horde of friends, an extensive wardrobe of gorgeous clothes, an exquisite figure, plus to top it all off, a generous heart and spirit. Everyone loved Amelie. What wasn't to love?

Erin sighed, knowing she'd never measure up.

Slipping on a pair of black strappy heels, Erin turned back to the mirror for one more glance. Her hand flew to her hair. What was she thinking? Her hair looked completely lifeless—dull, dry and lank didn't even begin to describe it. What would Amelie say if she rocked up looking like that? Her hair certainly wouldn't be a good advertisement for Amelie's salon and her place of work. Why hadn't she found the time today to get a conditioning treatment, a trim, and maybe a few foil highlights? Surely Lilly or Joel, the other stylists at the salon, could have squeezed her into their busy schedules. They always did each other's hair at work when things were quiet. Mentally chastising herself, she quickly swept her hair up into a messy bun, allowing a few loose strands to fall for effect. *There. Much better.* Dabbing on a bit more lipstick, she decided she'd pass muster. She grabbed her phone, ticket and clutch from her bedside table and legged it to the front door.

Damn.

She'd forgotten to order an Uber.

Flashing her driver's licence and ticket under the bouncer's nose, Erin entered the chic Nirvana Nightclub and squinted, adjusting to the semi-darkness. Was this grandiose or what? Luxurious fittings and furniture, glamorous mood lighting, elegantly dressed clientele. Wow, it sure was a far cry from the usual nightclubs she visited. No stale cigarette smoke, beer, sweat or cheap perfume reeking here. Erin smiled, absorbing the atmosphere. It was perfect. Trust Amelie to always come up trumps. As Maid-of-Honour for their cousin Chelsea's wedding, Amelie had insisted on organising the Hen's Night by herself. Somehow coaxing two hundred dollars for tickets from over fifty of Chelsea's family, friends and colleagues was a breeze for Amelie, too. She had a knack for things like that. Erin glanced down at her ticket, straining her eyes to read it in the dim lighting:

The Hottest Hen's Night in Town
Thursday 25th November 2021 at 9 pm
The Den
Nirvana Nightclub
$200
Covers entry fee, free-flowing mimosas and canapés
Plus—the hottest male revue in town!
Let's help Chelsea enjoy her last days of freedom!

The Den? She craned her neck and looked around. Where the hell was *The Den*? Probably downstairs somewhere, she decided. Edging her way around a crowded dance floor, she excused herself through a crowd of martini-sipping patrons, her eyes frantically scanning the room for a stairwell or a sign pointing her in the right direction. Passing the DJ booth, she finally spotted a black arrow on the wall with the words *The Den* painted in gold on it. Thank goodness! It was already twenty past nine. Amelie wasn't going to be impressed that she was late.

A good-looking guy with all the hallmarks of a

Hollywood hunk stood guard at the top of the stairs leading down to *The Den*, a chain draped across the entrance with a 'Private Function' sign swinging from its centre. Dressed in neat black pants and a snug-fitting white shirt that hugged his amazing physique, he was staring down at his phone. Looking up as Erin approached, his eyes widened, and his lips curled into a sexy smile.

'Hey,' he said.

'Hey yourself,' Erin couldn't help but smile back. 'Erin Barber.'

'Come again?'

'Erin Barber,' she pointed to his phone and flashed her ticket. 'For your attendee list. I'm here for Chelsea's Hen's Night. Downstairs in *The Den*, I believe.'

He cracked a big smile. A smokin' hot smile, in fact. His gaze dropped down to her dress—the dress she knew hugged her tightly in all the right places and left little to the imagination. His cobalt-blue eyes lit with an inner twinkle as they traced the outlines of her curves. He looked up and locked eyes with hers. *Oh my!* He was so goddamned good looking; her pulse zoomed from first gear straight into third.

'E R I N B A R B E R,' he tapped slowly on his phone. 'And what's your phone number, Erin?'

'Um, 049157…'

'It's okay. I was just kidding. I'm not checking off names. In fact, I don't even work here. But you can give me your number if you want to.' He cocked his head and grinned.

'Huh! In your dreams,' Erin said with a laugh, her heart doing a funny little dance in her chest. As she reached past him to unhitch the chain, their arms brushed together for a brief moment. Ignoring the tingling sensation of his skin on hers, she gave him a playful nudge, and he stepped back, his hand held up in surrender.

'Enjoy the Hen's Night, Erin,' he said.

Unable to hide the smile on her face, she raced down the stairs, resisting the urge to glance back up.

Cheeky bugger.

'About time!' Amelie raced across the room to greet her with a hug. 'The show starts in around ten minutes. We're already on our second or third drinks. You look great, by the way. But you're the last one to arrive, as usual.'

How did Amelie always manage to do that? Give a compliment with a reprimand attached? Maybe it was just a big sister thing. Erin forced herself to withhold a groan.

'Sorry I'm late. You look amazing, as usual. New dress?' Erin asked.

'What, this old thing? No, it was just sitting there in my closet. Felt it was time to give it an airing.' Amelie twirled around.

No doubt the gold dress cost more than Erin's monthly salary.

Erin glanced around the well-lit room. Absolutely perfect—cabaret-style layout, small round tables facing a stage with a closed black velvet curtain, a huge bar on one side and a dance floor on the other. Soft music, animated voices, laughter and clinking glasses filled the room.

Amelie grabbed her arm and dragged her towards the stage, blowing air kisses to various acquaintances as she went.

'We're at the front, centre table. Best view in the house. Wait until you see who's here,' Amelie said.

Chelsea leapt up from the table and enveloped Erin in a bear hug.

'Erin, you're here! I was starting to get worried,' she said.

'Oh my God, Chels. You look divine,' Erin said, 'Just love your jumpsuit. Fits you like a glove. You are going to be the most beautiful bride.'

'Aww, thanks Cuz. Look who's here.' Chelsea stepped aside to expose the mystery guest seated at their table.

'Gran? Wow! I never expected to see you here. This is so awesome. I didn't know you went to nightclubs, especially when there are bound to be male strippers in the dance revue,' Erin said with a grin.

She bent down and kissed Lizzie Barber on the top of her head.

'Well, you know me, I've never missed a family Hen's Night yet, so I sure as hell wasn't planning on missing this one. Who needs strippers, anyway? These g-string waiters are pretty good eye candy,' Lizzie said, waving one over to grab another mimosa from his tray.

'Gran!' Erin, Amelie and Chelsea cried out in unison.

'What?' Lizzie said, as a smile spread across her face. 'I'm eighty-five, not dead! I may still be married to your grandfather, but I can still go window-shopping, can't I?'

'Gran, you're incorrigible,' Amelie said, a look of mock horror on her face.

'Pfft, I bet you don't even know how to spell that word,' Lizzie said. 'Erin, grab yourself a drink from this fine young specimen of a man. In fact, take two—you've got to catch up with the rest of us.'

Erin grabbed a mimosa from the hovering

waiter, averting her gaze from his gold lamé g-string and focusing on his gold bow tie and bowler hat.

'Cute costumes, aren't they?' Lizzie said, giving him a wink as he walked away. She stood and twirled around in a circle.

'Well, girls,' she said, 'What do you think of your gran's new outfit?'

'Well, Gran,' Erin said. 'Nobody can rock skinny white jeggings and see-through shirts the way you can.'

'I know it's not my usual style, but I asked for advice at Lulu's Boutique today. I was told that everyone who goes to a Hen's Night these days wears a lot more makeup than usual and dresses a little more scantily than normal.' Lizzie roared with laughter, her eyes twinkling mischievously.

'Well, you know what they say, Gran. When in Rome, dress like a stripper!' Erin couldn't help but laugh with this beautiful woman who was always loud, always full of life, and always had the ability to laugh as if she was still sixteen years of age.

'You look fabulous.'

The lights dimmed as a statuesque blonde woman took to the stage, holding a cordless microphone in one hand, her other hand behind her back.

'Ladies, please take your seats so we can get this show on the road,' she said. 'My name is Minka, and I'm your hostess tonight. Firstly, let me welcome you all here to celebrate Chelsea's Hen's Night. Let's all give Chelsea a huge round of applause.'

Chelsea's face erupted into a huge grin as the room filled with clapping and cheering. She stood, turned around to face everyone and gave an over-the-top curtsy.

'Thanks heaps, guys,' she yelled.

'Now,' Minka continued, 'I believe tonight's organiser, the lovely Amelie, has kept the details of the show a big secret. Well, it's now time to let the cat out of the bag, ladies! Because tonight we have a really hot, really exciting show for you. So, make sure you all have plenty of those nice cool mimosas on hand to cool you down, 'cos once you see the super-hot dudes lined up backstage, you're going to need them!'

Screams and thunderous applause filled the room.

'Woohoo! Bring 'em on!' Lizzie shouted.

Erin glanced at her grandmother and laughed. Maybe age really was just a number, and being an octogenarian was something to look forward to.

Minka continued, 'Tonight's dance revue, ladies, is performed by twelve of Perth's hottest pin-up guys. That's right, ladies, they are, in fact, the twelve fireys who are gracing next year's *WA Firefighters' Calendar.*'

She removed her hand from behind her back, held up a calendar, and was instantly greeted with a cacophony of whoops. The mimosas were certainly doing their job.

'Not only are these amazing fellas generously donating their time to promote this venture, but they also went and learnt a whole dance show to earn more money for their quest. Tonight, fifty percent of your ticket price is being donated to their fundraising cause—raising money for the Burns Unit at the new Children's Hospital. After the show, I'll have a special announcement. But for now, sit back, kick your shoes off, drink up, eat yourselves silly and enjoy… *The Blazing Hotshots*.'

Music blasted from the speakers, and the heavy curtain opened to expose twelve extremely hunky men standing in different poses—identically dressed in skin-tight denim jeans, white singlets with their month names printed across the front— singlets that looked like they were painted directly onto their well-defined six-packs. Cowboy boots and hats completed their outfits.

'Well, set my house on fire!' Lizzie yelled, leaping out of her chair and clapping like a crazy woman.

'Gran!' Her three granddaughters dragged her back to her chair, laughing.

The audience went berserk. Squeals of excitement filled the room. Phone cameras flashed like crazy as the men launched into a positively electrifying tap routine, showcasing their strength and power. With impeccable timing, they busted out moves that were not only sexy but rugged, raw and edgy. The tap routine ended to a raucous standing ovation—the ladies going wild, screaming for more. The fireys launched straight into a second routine, followed quickly by a third, then a fourth, exhibiting flawless synchronisation, each sending the crowd even wilder.

Erin was gobsmacked. How could these guys be so lithe and so athletic at the same time? Surely, they were real dancers, not fireys? She glanced at her gran, dancing in her seat and whooping with the best of them. Erin grinned. Was there no limit to this amazing woman's energy?

'Move over, Dein Perry,' Lizzie yelled loudly, 'These guys are hotter than Tap Dogs!'

'Dean who?' Erin asked.

'Never mind, love, these guys can park their tap shoes under my bed anytime. Just don't tell your grandfather,' Lizzie said, zipping her lips with her fingers. 'Pick a favourite, Erin. I'm leaning towards Mr April.'

'Um, gosh, I don't know. Mr November, I think. He reminds me of someone. He's rather hot, don't you think? Look at those muscles straining against his singlet. He's certainly got bulges in all the right places!' Erin said with a laugh.

'Atta girl,' Lizzie grinned, patting Erin on the arm.

The fourth tap routine ended—the music quickly changing to a slower pace. The song from *The Full Monty* caused an uproar from the crowd. Velcro-joined singlets were ripped off during the routine and hurled into the crowd. Lizzie caught one and hugged it tightly to her chest. The stage spotlights dimmed as jeans were also ripped off and tossed side-stage with one hand. The other hand simultaneously removed the cowboy hats to quickly cover shiny-gold g-strings as the song ended.

Now standing on her chair, Lizzie was cheering and yelling, 'Noooo, don't leave your hats on!'

'Gran, get down. Keep your knickers on!' Erin said as tears of laughter rolled down her cheeks. 'You'll fall and break a hip. Or have a heart attack.' Her voice was hoarse from screaming, but she was loving every moment.

The curtain closed, and Minka appeared back on the stage.

'Wow, was that insane or what?' she shouted. 'I have a sneaky suspicion that you all enjoyed that. Ladies, please give it up for *The Blazing Hotshots*!'

As soon as the applause died down, the curtain re-opened and standing on the stage were all twelve men, now dressed in open-chested overalls, boots and fire helmets.

'Now, ladies,' Minka said, 'I have some good news for you all. These super-hot, super talented firefighters, and yes ladies, they are all bona fide, genuine fireys from fire stations all over the metro area… have offered themselves to be the prizes in a silent auction to allow one of you lovely ladies to win a dinner-date. The highest bidder tonight will spend a lovely meal with the firey of her choice. Shortly, they'll come down to mingle and give you all a complimentary calendar. Once you know your favourite, you can head to the table at the back and place your silent bid. The money from the highest bidder will be donated to the Children's Burns Unit. How amazing is that? So, what are you all waiting for?'

'Five hundred for Mr April,' someone yelled from the back of the room.

'I said it's a *silent* auction, ladies,' Minka laughed, shaking her head, as the lights in the room grew brighter.

'Go put a bid on, Erin,' Lizzie said. 'Who did you fancy again, Mr November, wasn't it?'

'God no, I can't afford it. That girl up the back just said five hundred. I just forked out two hundred bucks for tonight's ticket. I'm only a trainee hairdresser, remember. We get paid bugger-all!' Erin said, rolling her eyes at Amelie.

'Let's all go and mingle and meet some hot fireys, maybe hit the dance floor,' Chelsea said, grabbing Amelie's and Erin's arms and pulling them out of their seats. 'You too, Gran.'

'I'll be there in a sec,' Lizzie said. 'Just need to nip to the Ladies. Bloody bladder is the size of a pea these days.'

'I'll be over in a sec too,' Erin said, sitting back down. 'Just want to check the photos I took of the show. Might upload a few to Insta.'

'Don't be long,' Chelsea said with Amelie in tow, disappearing into the throng behind them.

Erin scrolled through her photo gallery. Wow, had she really taken this many? So many to choose from. How could anyone pick a favourite? They were all hot and as sexy as hell. Yep, sure, Mr April was pretty hot—his tousled dirty-blonde locks with that *just out of bed* look and his dark green *come-hither* eyes were certainly mesmerising and alluring. But there was something strangely familiar about Mr November that she couldn't quite put her finger on. Something drew her to him. She stretched the screen wide to zoom in. Wait. No! Surely not? Is he the Hollywood hunk from upstairs? How come she was only just noticing this? She'd had her eyes glued on him for over thirty minutes while he was on stage, but that cowboy hat had obviously partially obscured his face.

'Excuse me, is this seat taken?'

Erin looked up and forced herself not to suck in a deep breath. There he was, standing in front of her in all his bare-chested glory—Mr November— flashing her a drop-dead gorgeous smile. His eyes locked with hers, causing her stomach to tie up in knots. She dropped her gaze before the intensity grew too much. Unfortunately, it dropped straight to his amazing six-pack—his spectacular upper torso barely covered by the open overalls. Heat rushed to her cheeks, and her heart was pounding so fast that she suddenly seemed incapable of stringing a sentence together.

'Um, yes… I mean no, I don't think so. Not now.'

He pointed to the empty chair.

'May I?' he asked as his smile reached his eyes.

Erin swallowed the lump that had welled in her throat and simply nodded.

'It's Erin if I remember correctly, isn't it? Erin… Barber? Um, let me see now, 049157… but hey, you never did get around to giving me the rest.

You can put it in my phone now if you like.' He offered her his phone and gave her a cheeky grin.

She stared at his outstretched arm and then lifted her gaze back to stare stupidly at Mr November, her mouth slightly agape. Was this really happening? A super-hot, real-life firefighter was asking for *her* number? Things like this didn't happen to girls like her. He smiled again—a smile that filled his eyes with a mischievous twinkle—a smile that somehow seemed to untangle and calm her nerves.

'My phone number, eh? Wow, that's stretching a friendship,' she said, the corners of her mouth curving upwards as her brain finally engaged with her mouth.

'Good start. I just sat down one minute ago, and we already have a friendship. How cool is that? Looks like my irresistible charm is working,' he said with a wink. 'So, Erin, my new friend, my name's Cole.'

He smiled at her again—a smile that instantly caused the blood to start humming in her veins.

'Hi,' was all she could manage.

'And what, pray tell, did you think of our show?' Cole said. 'Judging by the screams, you all seemed to enjoy it. Oh, and who was that awesome older lady from this table, the one that was up on the chair? The one that was really going for it. Your mother?'

'Ha!' Erin said. 'You'll be her friend for life if she hears you say that. She's our grandmother. My mother wouldn't be seen dead in a nightclub.'

'Cool, another instant friend. I'll make a point of telling her. I'm on a roll tonight.' He pretended to tap on his phone. 'Erin's nanna. Wonder if *she'll* give me her number?'

'Knowing Gran, I'd say it was on the cards.' Erin giggled. How could he be so cute, so hot, and so obnoxiously endearing at the same time?

'Hey, you wanna dance? I'm all fired up, ready to go. Pardon the pun.' He stood, extending his hand, not waiting for an answer.

Erin's cheeks warmed again. Surely, he'd regret asking her when he found out she had two left feet and no rhythm. But he was so goddamned good looking; how could she refuse?

He grabbed her hand to lead her to where the action was. The touch of his skin against hers instantly caused her stomach to do a backflip.

Chelsea, Amelie and a swarm of other young ladies were in the middle of the dance floor, whirling and whooping with a few of the fireys. Chelsea winked at Erin, mouthing a 'Wow!' as they joined the dance floor. Cole immediately started performing incredible dance moves. It wasn't fair that some people were natural-born dancers. He pulled Erin closer. Tingles ricocheted down her spine as his musky scent created an acute surge of desire. Wait, no, it was a musky-citrus scent. Was that even a thing? As the thrumming rhythm of the music started to pulse within her, Erin tried her best to follow his lead. Within minutes, her jitters melted. As the beat picked up the pace, she found a sudden burst of courage and started busting out moves she'd never tried before—moves she never knew she held within. Deciding there was nothing to lose, she danced her inhibitions away.

After a while, the music stopped, the spotlight shone once again on the stage, and Minka reappeared.

'Can I please ask all the fireys to come back on stage so I can announce the winner of the silent auction?' she said.

'Thanks for the dances, Erin,' Cole said, his voice soft and raw. He leaned forward and brushed his lips against hers in a feather-like kiss, catching Erin by surprise.

Wow, I wasn't expecting that.

Smiling, she floated back down from cloud nine and headed back to the table to join the others.

'Firstly,' Minka said, 'The firey who won the highest bid tonight is… drum roll please… none other than the super-hot, the super-sexy, Mr November, aka Cole Buchanan from the Appleby Fire Station. Ladies, please, give it up for Mr November.'

Raucous applause filled the room. Erin's heart instantly deflated like a balloon with a pinprick.

Damn! Sometimes it would be nice to be flush with money. She glanced around her, wondering who the lucky lady was.

Chelsea gave her a nudge. 'Wow, Erin! How cool is that? He's gorgeous! I saw you two on the dance floor. And he's a local too. You go, girl!'

'Now, Cole,' Minka continued, 'The bid was an amazing amount—three thousand dollars, in fact! One of these gorgeous ladies has promised to pay that amount to the fundraiser for a dinner date with you. A dinner at *Maxwell's on the Terrace*, by the way, Perth's hottest new restaurant. They have donated a three-course dinner with drinks included. So now, ladies, I'll give Cole this envelope, and he can announce the winning bidder's name.'

Stepping forward and taking the microphone and the envelope, Cole slowly opened it, dropping his gaze briefly to the slip of paper. A smile crept across his face. His eyes scanned the room, purposely looking every lady in the eye, drawing out the suspense. Finally, his gaze fixated on Erin.

'Erin Barber,' he said loudly, giving her a

cheeky wink.

Suddenly, the air in the room grew heavy, making it hard for Erin to breathe. Her throat tightened just as the almost-full mimosa glass slipped from her fingers and smashed on the floor.

'Wait… what?' she stammered. 'I didn't… this has got to be a mistake! Amelie?'

'Don't look at me,' her sister replied with a laugh. 'I love you to bits, but I don't love you that much.'

'Wasn't me either,' Chelsea said with a grin. 'I'm poor. I've got a wedding to pay for.'

All three girls turned quickly towards Lizzie, who was toying with her drink.

'Gran?' they called out in unison.

'What?' Lizzie sheepishly replied, trying her hardest to be the face of innocence but somehow not managing to hide the mischievous twinkle in her eyes.

'Oh my God, Gran,' Erin said as her hand flew to her mouth. 'What the hell have you done?'

Erin awoke with a monster headache. She groaned and rolled over, cocooning herself under the doona. Her head pounded, her stomach churned, and her throat was parched. She closed her eyes and slowly rubbed her temples. Who in their right mind organises a Hen's Night on a weeknight knowing full well that everyone has to get up the next day and go to work? Amelie, that's who. Well, serves her right if Erin was late. She had no intention of getting out of bed yet.

She dozed for a while longer, her dreams filled with crazy images of her gran dancing with lots of sexy half-dressed firefighters. Erin's eyes flew open. Oh my God!

Gran.

The crafty old devil.

'I did it for you, darling,' Lizzie had said. 'You obviously like each other. You can't deny it—I saw you on the dance floor. And it's time you had someone in your life. Chelsea's about to get married to Ben, and Amelie has Anton. Besides, it's just a dinner date. What's the harm in that?'

'But Gran, three thousand dollars? Seriously, that's a shitload of money,' Erin had replied.

'All for a good cause, love,' was Lizzie's comeback.

Erin finally stumbled out of bed in search of Panadol and coffee. The pain in her head hadn't subsided one iota, and the thought of food made her stomach recoil. She vowed never to drink mimosas ever again. Whoever said a twenty-five-minute warm shower wouldn't do wonders for a hangover obviously didn't know what they were talking about. Finally, Erin was in a fit state to head off to work.

Arriving at the hair salon forty-five minutes late, Erin breezed through the front door as if she owned the place.

'Good afternoon, Miss Barber,' Anton called across the salon. He moved a pair of scissors across a client's fringe in delicate and precise motions. 'So glad that you have decided to grace us with your presence today.'

Being the head stylist, Anton was the most requested staff member for haircuts, especially when the client wanted a chic new look. Anton's styles were always in vogue; he kept up with the latest trends from around the world. Most days, Erin looked up to him, admired his talents and absorbed his every word.

Today, she simply cursed under her breath. She bit the inside of her cheek to keep her tongue in check.

'Erin,' Amelie said as she rushed over. 'You're so late! You need to get everything ready for Mrs Anderson's perm. You were meant to be here ages ago. Go out the back and get the rods and papers. Get mostly red rods and some blues... she has a small curl, remember. Don't stuff it up. And make sure the rubbers on the rods are okay... if not, grab a new box from the storeroom. Oh, and a bottle of that new brand of neutraliser—grab one of those too. Earth to Erin! Why are you just standing there?'

Erin sighed. Why would Amelie ask her to do a perm? Today of all days. Surely, she should have known that Erin would have a hangover after a huge night like last night. Plus, she knew Erin hated doing perms. Who the hell has perms in this day and age anyway? God only knows why they still teach it at the Academy.

'I feel fine, Amelie. Thanks for asking! Are there any painkillers in the kitchen?' Erin said. 'I need some before I can do anything.'

'I've got some in my bag,' Lilly said as she approached the front reception desk. 'Come with me.'

Erin followed Lilly to the staff lunchroom. She grabbed a couple of painkillers from Lilly, filled a huge tumbler with water, and swallowed the tablets.

'Oh, my aching head!' Erin moaned, once again rubbing her temples. 'I'm never drinking again.'

'So, you little minx, I heard all about last night from Amelie. How exciting, Erin! I saw your

Instagram posts, and oh my God, he is one smoking-hot dude. When's the big date?' Lilly said.

'Tomorrow night, would you believe? I don't even know if I want to go. But Gran donated three bloody thousand dollars, so what choice do I have? I mean, sure, he's hot and gorgeous, but why would he even want to go on a date with someone like me? I know he probably doesn't have a choice. It's all part of the fundraising. But still… poor guy.'

'Nah, I bet he'll love it. You'll both have a ball. It's supposed to be a really classy restaurant, too… with amazing food. So, what are you wearing?' Lilly said.

A bead of sweat broke out on Erin's forehead. Her eyes rolled upwards as she let out a breath she hadn't realised she'd been holding.

'That's just it, Lilly. I have nothing suitable to wear. Plus, my bank account is almost empty, and my credit card maxed out, so I can't even go shopping tomorrow.'

'*Der*! Don't you have a sister with an extensive, amazing wardrobe full of stylish clothes? Bet she has a few hot little numbers! And you're almost the same size… well maybe, you're a tad bigger in the cup size, but you'll find something. Don't stress. Do you want a hand putting new rubbers on these perm rods? They look a bit manky,' Lilly said.

Erin sat back in the plush burgundy chair, a wine glass in her hand. She was enjoying her second glass. Why did she always threaten to never drink again after every hangover? Somehow a glass of wine always seemed to calm her nerves when she was feeling anxious. Feeling anxious? That was an understatement. Sitting in one of the poshest new restaurants in town on her own—most likely stood-up—was enough to drive anyone to drink. Sensing the staff were talking about her in hushed tones, Erin's cheeks warmed. How embarrassing, winning a hot date with someone who can't even be bothered showing up.

Placing her now-empty wine glass back on the table, she fished her phone out of Amelie's borrowed Oroton clutch to check for a message. Nothing. Nil. Nada. She'd exchanged numbers with Cole before leaving *The Den*, so there was no excuse. Should she phone him? It was already after eight-thirty, and Cole had arranged to meet her at the restaurant at eight o'clock. For once in her life, Erin had arrived a full ten minutes early.

She picked up the menu for the sixth time and, for the sixth time, creased her forehead. What the hell was all this stuff? Langoustine with a shellfish and black truffle velouté topped with a delicate pepper tuile? She was more a pulled-pork burger girl herself. A waiter suddenly appeared and motioned towards the wine bottle she'd ordered. Erin nodded. The wine was already going to her head, but she may as well have a third glass before she discreetly slipped out of the restaurant.

'Starting without me, I see.'

Erin spun her head around and instantly sucked in her breath. Dressed in an immaculately tailored black suit, complete with a crisp white shirt and black bow tie, Cole would be a sure-fire winner in the search for a new James Bond actor. Despite wearing one of Amelie's little black numbers, by some famous Aussie designer whose name she couldn't remember, Erin suddenly felt underdressed.

'Sorry I'm so late,' Cole said, bending down and brushing her cheek with his lips. 'I had an emergency. I should have texted or called, but I didn't think it would take that long. Sorry.'

A wave of relief washed over Erin. How embarrassing would it have been if she *had* been stood up? She smiled at Cole as he accepted a glass of wine from the hovering waiter and nodded his thanks. Who would have thought she'd ever end up on a date with such a smoking hot guy?

'Cheers,' Cole said, raising his glass to Erin. She instantly grabbed hers, and they clinked glasses. 'Mm, this is really good. You chose well, whatever it is. I'm not much of a wine buff myself, to be honest.'

Cole placed his wine glass down on the table and fiddled with his bow tie.

'Hey, doesn't this place look amazing?' Cole scanned the room before settling his gaze back on Erin. 'Erin, I feel so bad about being late, but sometimes these things happen. Forgive me?'

Erin had been staring unabashedly at him

without uttering one word. Whatever pent-up annoyance she had surging through her veins a few minutes ago had now completely flown out of the window. She couldn't believe she was on a dinner date with such a hot guy. In fact, he was so goddamned good-looking she suddenly had the strangest urge to… wait, what? Where did that naughty thought come from? It must be the wine. They'd only just met a couple of days ago. Even Gran would be shocked if she could read Erin's mind right now, and nothing shocked Gran. Erin needed to put those thoughts out of her head once and for all. This was just a charity dinner date, nothing more, nothing less. A one-off thing. Besides, she didn't really want to do those wicked things to Cole, but… oh, who the hell was she trying to kid? Of course, she did.

'Erin, are you okay? You look a bit… dazed.' Cole reached across the table and placed his hand on top of hers.

Electricity zinged between them. Erin stifled the moan threatening to seep out. Had he felt that too? Surely that wasn't one-sided? She took a deep breath. She had to stop staring at him, or he'd probably think she had a giant-sized crush on him, like a love-struck teenager fresh out of school.

'Um, yeah, I'm fine, thanks. Sorry, I think I drank the first two glasses of wine too quickly. You know—empty stomachs and alcohol are a recipe for disaster. And no worries about being late. I guess emergencies crop up all the time in your line of work.'

'Yeah, you could say that,' Cole said, now scanning the menu. 'Wow, have you checked this out? This looks incredible. Expensively incredible, but still. What are you fancying?'

Ha! Isn't it obvious?

She handed Cole her menu and giggled. 'Why don't you choose for me? I'm not really used to fancy food like this. But I'm game to try anything. Surprise me.'

A playful smile created a mischievous twinkle in Cole's eyes.

'Ah! The lady likes surprises. Good to know. Gosh, look at this menu—so much to choose from.

How's your schoolgirl French?' Cole laughed as he waved to a passing waiter. 'Um, let's see. We'll both start with this one, the Boo… Booey…'

'The Bouillabaisse, sir?'

'That's it! And for the main, we'll have… er… Magret de Canard. Thank you.'

'And for dessert, sir?'

'We'll decide later, thanks,' Cole said, handing the menus to the waiter. 'But hey, before you go, would you mind taking a few photos of us? We'll be sure to promote the restaurant on social media. Thanks.'

Cole handed his phone to the waiter, who tucked his order pad under his arm. Moving his chair around to Erin's side of the table, Cole put his arm around her shoulders and pecked her on the cheek.

'Smile,' the waiter said.

Despite the electric tingles she was experiencing, Erin gave her most brilliant smile for the shots.

'Magret de Canard. Did I pronounce that

correctly? Sounds impressive,' Erin said as Cole moved his chair back. 'So, what exactly will we be eating?'

'I have absolutely no idea. But at seventy-five dollars each for the entrée and one-hundred-and-twenty-five dollars for the mains when we're not paying, who cares?' Cole's face erupted into a wonderfully wicked grin. 'So, Erin Barber, tell me a bit about yourself. You already know I'm a firey, but I have absolutely no idea what you do, or anything about you, except that you've got an awesome, wealthy and generous grandmother and a cousin getting married soon.'

'Well,' Erin took a sip of her wine. 'There's not much to tell, really. I'm nineteen, almost twenty, single, a trainee hairdresser—but I've almost finished my apprenticeship. And I work in my sister Amelie's salon in Appleby, on Sheffield Street. Well, it's her and her boyfriend's salon, to be precise. And that's me in a nutshell. Boring, plain, old Erin.'

'Oh, come on,' Cole said. 'You're not boring, and geez, you're certainly not old. Not like me, I'm almost twenty-five. And plain? Who are you trying to kid? You're one of the prettiest girls I've been on a date with for ages. Seriously! But what about your hobbies, interests? I know you like dancing— you were pretty cool strutting your stuff on the dance floor the other night.'

'Ha! Are you kidding? That was the mimosas dancing. I have two left feet.'

'Well, I'd be pretty happy to dance with your mimosas any old time,' Cole said with a wink. 'And what a coincidence—we both work in Appleby. I think I've seen that hair salon. It's near that Italian pizza bar and the gelato shop, isn't it?'

'Yep,' Erin grinned. 'That gelato shop is my favourite go-to lunch bar. I think I'm their best customer. The pizza shop's not bad, either.'

'There you go, that's two more things I learned about you—you love gelato and pizza! Wow, looks like this is our entrée coming. That was quick. Hope it's good.'

Erin looked down at the large flat bowl placed in front of her. Her brow knitted into a frown.

What the hell was this stuff? It smelled fishy but also had a citrusy smell with a hint of aniseed. Weird combination. Chunks of white fish flesh, squid rings, scallops, prawns and several black mussel shells floated in an amber liquid. Did it require a knife and fork, a soup spoon, or all three? She had no idea. There was so much cutlery in front of her that she had to follow Cole's lead. Fork it apparently was, then.

She pushed the pieces of seafood around the bowl with her fork, finally stabbing a piece of fish and tentatively put it in her mouth. How could something that cost seventy-five dollars taste so disgusting? She swallowed without chewing and washed it down with two big gulps of wine. How could she finish eating this without physically being sick? Beads of sweat broke out on her forehead as her stomach started complaining.

'You don't actually have to eat it, you know,' Cole said as he shovelled a large prawn into his mouth. 'I have to say, it has got a weird flavour. Do you want to order something else?'

Erin put her fork down and pushed the bowl

away. 'I'm sorry. I think I've had too much wine to actually enjoy food. My stomach's in a swirl.'

Cole looked up, fork mid-air and grinned at Erin.

'Hey, you wanna get out of here? Maybe head to the beach for a walk in the moonlight or a dip in the ocean? Pick up a couple of burgers on the way? The fresh air will do you good.'

'But we haven't had the mains yet… and Gran paid a fortune for me to be here tonight.'

'I'll just tell the waiter to cancel them. I'll say you're not feeling well or something. Besides, we got the obligatory promo photos. What do you say?'

'Well, you're a bit overdressed for the beach, and we don't have any bathing suits for a swim, but hey, I say, let's do it,' Erin said with a laugh. 'As long as you don't spill the beans to Gran. Oh, my goodness, she would not be impressed.'

Cole jumped up quickly and raced around to pull Erin's chair out. As he grabbed her arm, the electric sparks charged through her again.

Oh my!

'Anyway, who said we need bathing suits for a swim?' Cole's eyes were filled to the brim with cheekiness.

Erin stared at the peacefully sleeping Cole. Had last night really happened? A barefoot walk along a deserted beach, under a star-filled night sky, was the most romantic thing she'd ever done. They'd talked as they walked—about nothing and yet about everything. She had felt so comfortable in his presence. Erin hadn't been able to stop her heart from beating at a million miles an hour when Cole had asked if he could kiss her. How could she refuse? He was, beyond a doubt, the most devilishly handsome guy she'd ever been on a date with.

At first, his kiss was soft and gentle, but then it deepened into a kiss full of powerful intensity, like no kiss she'd ever experienced before. His insistent mouth had parted her lips, his teasing tongue dancing over hers. The surging tide of warmth from his kiss sent wild tremors throughout her body, causing several moans to escape from within.

Somehow, they'd ended up here, in her apartment. And oh, what a night! Erin's appreciative gaze ran down Cole's trim, taut and terrific body—his naked body—causing wicked thoughts to fill her mind. Lying face down, he continued sleeping peacefully, even after Erin jumped out of bed in search of coffee.

Reaching for two mugs, she was suddenly startled by footsteps. Turning around, she grinned at Cole standing in the doorway to the kitchen, wrapped in a sheet.

'Good morning. Would you like some coffee?' Erin beamed.

'No thanks. What I want is for you to come back to bed,' Cole said as he dropped the sheet to the floor.

'Yes, Gran, we had an amazing dinner date. I honestly don't know how to thank you. Yes, Cole is absolutely gorgeous,' Erin said, holding her mobile phone close to her ear. 'The food? Oh, well, it was very different to my usual taste and super expensive. Mostly French cuisine, I think. I couldn't even pronounce what we ate. No, we skipped dessert. Yes, that's right, I'm sweet enough.'

Besides, I'd swap a piece of French gateau for a night of wild abandon any day.

'Was he what? A complete gentleman? Of course, Gran.'

Ha! I'm so glad he wasn't. If only you knew!

'Yes, he wants to catch up again. He suggested next Saturday night because he's rostered on all week. Yes, I know, that's Chelsea's wedding. So, guess who now has a Plus-One?'

Erin slumped down onto a pew at the back of St Jerome's church. Fishing her phone from her clutch for the umpteenth time, she noticed it was now five minutes to four. Still no messages. The wedding service was due to start at four, but hopefully, Chelsea would be fashionably late, allowing Cole time to get here and slide into the back pew beside her.

The church quickly filled; guests were being shown to the correct side of the church by the usher. Erin noticed her gran giving her worrying looks, so she just waved back, smiled and shrugged. This was going to be mega embarrassing if Cole didn't show up. It was probably another emergency—yes, that would be it. Fire-fighters were always on call, weren't they? Erin had been singing Cole's praises to anyone who would listen all week long. She dreaded everyone thinking she'd been stood up and the whole thing had been nothing more than a one-night-stand.

The organist suddenly lurched into playing Mendelssohn's Wedding March, and the congregation stood. A deep sigh escaped from Erin's lungs. Looks like she'd be minus a Plus-One after all—the poor old family singleton, yet again. She turned towards the doorway to watch as the junior bridesmaids entered, followed by Amelie—looking absolutely stunning in a nude-coloured, floor-length, simple, figure-hugging gown. Chelsea followed, accompanied by her father. Chelsea looked breathtakingly radiant in her sleek white satin gown—the exact way Erin hoped to look one day when the time came.

Erin's gaze remained on the open doorway after the bridal party entered, hoping against hope that Cole would come rushing in at the last minute. The usher quietly closed the door. Erin sighed again. It was going to be a long, miserable night.

'So, how was the wedding?' Lilly cornered Erin in the staff lunchroom first thing on Monday morning. 'I didn't see any hot and steamy photos of you and Mr November on Instagram. Too busy to post any—nudge, nudge?'

'The wedding was nice, I guess. But Cole was a no-show,' Erin said as she sipped a mug of coffee. 'And, he hasn't had the courtesy of replying to my texts to explain. I must have sent over twenty messages yesterday. He's ghosted me. What a jerk. Guess he was really only after a one-night stand. More fool me!'

'Oh, Erin, I am so sorry,' Lilly said. 'I was kind of hoping you two would get it together. Those promo photos of you two at Maxwell's on social media last week were adorable. You make such a cute couple.'

'Made. Not make. Past tense,' Erin said, hugging the warm coffee mug to her chest.

'Erin, you're wanted at the reception desk,' Joel called through the doorway.

'Bugger, Gran must be early for her colour. I was hoping to finish my coffee first,' Erin said, tipping over half a mug of the hot liquid down the sink. 'She's the last person I want to see. She wasted three thousand dollars because of me. I tried so hard to avoid her at the reception. Oh well, here goes—wish me luck.' She walked slowly out into the salon, wishing she'd called in sick—spending the day watching Netflix and wallowing in self-pity is what she really craved.

She stopped dead in her tracks. Standing on the other side of the reception desk was Cole, his snug white t-shirt straining against his biceps and chest, his gorgeous face lit up in a big grin.

'Cole,' she whispered, fighting off the urge to fly across the reception desk and punch him.

'Hello,' a little tiny voice said.

Erin peered over the desk to find the cutest little girl, who looked about four, standing beside Cole, holding his hand.

'Erin, I'm so, so sorry about Saturday,' Cole said. 'Something cropped up very urgently and unexpectantly, so I couldn't make it to the wedding. To make matters worse, I've lost my phone, so I didn't have your number to text or call you with an explanation.'

With one eyebrow raised, Erin glared at him.

'You forgot where I lived too, did you? You couldn't have come around yesterday to explain? Or sent word to the reception? You knew where it was.' Erin's raised voice caused the other staff to look up from attending to their clients.

Anton glared.

Amelie shook her head.

Erin peered down again at the little girl, who was tugging at Cole's arm impatiently.

'Are you the nice lady who's going to cut my hair?' the little girl asked, giving Erin the sweetest smile—a smile that reached her eyes. Eyes that looked exactly like… Cole's.

Erin's gaze bounced between Cole and the girl.

'Who—' Erin started to speak.

'Sorry, this is Bella. Bella, this is Erin, and I certainly *hope* she's the nice lady who will cut your hair,' Cole said, flashing a smile at Erin. A smile that, for once, fell flat.

'Daddy said I have to have a haircut today because Mummy is bringing our new baby home from hospital, and we're going to have special photos taken,' Bella said. 'Mummy got a brand-new baby sister for me on Saturday, but they can come home today, can't they?' Bella looked up at Cole.

Mummy. The word sliced through Erin, shredding her heart to pieces.

'That's right, Bella,' Cole said. 'It's going to be such an exciting day.'

Erin's throat closed up. How could she have been so stupid? She never actually asked Cole if he was single or married, and he had failed to mention it. Why hadn't it come up in their many hours of conversation? And bringing the child in to get his one-night-stand to give her a haircut? The cheek of the man. Erin realised she was frowning—a frown that was deepening by the second. How could he even think this was okay?

'Well, *do* you think you can fit her in? Please, Erin? Just a trim would be fine,' Cole said. 'We can wait a while if you're busy.'

Erin's chest tightened, and her lungs couldn't seem to inhale any air.

'No, sorry. I can't. I've got to go. Joel, can you come and assist these customers, please?' Erin called out as she fled the salon, through the back door via the staff lunchroom, grabbing her bag on the way. Running down the back alleyway towards the gelato shop, moisture gathered in her eyes as the sting of the situation stabbed her heart. What a complete fool she was.

Ordering a double serve of strawberry pistachio gelato, Erin slid silently into a booth at the rear of the shop. Again, tears pricked at her eyes, and she tried to blink them away. She didn't want to break down in public.

Lost in her miserable thoughts, Erin absentmindedly stabbed at her gelato with a spoon. Suddenly the sweet ice-cream aroma was overpowered… by a musky-citrus smell.

'Erin.'

The voice was unmistakable.

Cole.

Erin glanced up to find him standing beside her booth, his eyes searching hers.

'What the hell's going on? Why did you run away?' he asked.

'Leave me alone, Cole. I have nothing to say to you.' Erin gave him a long, pained look, then turned away.

'Can I please sit down? I want to emphasise how sorry I am. Truly, truly sorry,' he said.

Tilting her head up towards him, Erin's expression clouded. As tears started to form, she swiped at her eyes with the back of her hand.

'Didn't you forget something?' she asked, peering around him.

'Huh?'

'Your kid. Where's Bella?' she spat out the words as a painful tightness strangled her throat.

'What? Oh, Erin! That's what this is all about? You think Bella is my daughter?' Cole let out a huge sigh as he nervously ran his hand through his hair. 'Do you honestly think I'd keep that from you? I know we've only had one date and one night together, but Erin, I honestly would never have done either of those if I hadn't been completely, one hundred percent single and unattached.'

Erin turned her head away, swiping at her tears once more.

'Erin, please look at me. Give me the chance to explain. *Please.*'

Sighing, Erin reluctantly swung her head back towards him.

'Bella is my twin brother Emmett's daughter. His wife Hayley went into early labour on Saturday, and they had nobody available to mind Bella, so they dropped her off at my place with no warning. I had no choice but to stay home and look after her. She's been with me since. I'm not very good with kids, so it's been a steep learning curve. I honestly have no idea what I'm doing, but

Emmett thought a nice haircut for the baby's homecoming photos would be a great idea—and I agreed—especially because it would give me a chance to see you and explain my absence on Saturday. And I honestly have lost my phone. Please say you'll forgive me.'

Erin sat motionless, staring at him, twisting a loose tendril of her hair around her finger. Her mouth opened, but no words formed. Eventually, she slid across the bench seat, making room for Cole to sit. How stupid did she feel now? He must think she was a super-jealous nutcase.

Cole reached across and lightly grazed her cheek with his thumb, causing her heart rate to go into overdrive. Why did his touch always affect her like that? He hooked a finger under her chin and raised it, leaving her no choice but to gaze into his eyes—eyes that pulled her into an abyss of emotion, causing her breath to hitch.

Pulling her closer, his lips gently teased hers. He gave her a playful nudge and leaned back.

'Forgive me?' he asked, his eyebrows raised. 'I really want to see where this thing we've got going takes us. I want to spend more time with you and get to know you better.'

Wait… what? He thought they had a *thing*? Already? Was he falling for her? Was she falling for him? Her mind was in a spin. An overwhelming desire to kiss him took hold, and she laced her fingers through his belt loops and pulled him close.

'How could I not forgive those huge puppy-dog eyes?' she said. Her lips found his, at first covering them with feather-like kisses. Her teeth playfully bit his lower lip, causing Cole to moan quietly. His mouth claimed hers, parting her lips with a sense of urgency. The kiss deepened, sending Erin's heart into overdrive. A pleasurable ache flooded her body, and a strange, distant buzzing filled her ears.

'You'd better get that,' Cole said, pulling away, a grin on his face. 'It's obviously not my phone.'

Erin rummaged through her bag, scooping out her phone.

'It's just a text from Amelie. She said Bella's

fine, her haircut is finished, and Bella would like us to bring some ice-cream back. Apparently, Gran is reading her a magazine in the lunchroom. Knowing Gran, it's probably *Cosmopolitan*. I wonder how Amelie knew I was here getting ice-cream?'

'Your gran. She obviously knows you like the back of her hand. She rocked up just as you left and pointed me to the gelato shop. She told me to "go get my girl".'

'Your girl? I think I like the sound of that,' Erin's cheeks glowed. 'Um, but maybe we'd better head back now?'

Cole pulled her close again, his voice low against her ear.

'Not so fast, young lady.'

Hungrily seeking her lips once more, his kiss was filled with a raging fire that took her breath away. A raging fire that could not even be doused by a slightly-melted, double scoop of strawberry pistachio gelato—shared—with one spoon.

The End

About Jenny

Despite continually describing herself as a

fledgling writer, Jenny Lynch is notching successes faster than anybody can say 'Call the editor.' Publications of her flash fiction, short stories, quirky rhymes and novelettes, are certainly proving her wrong.

After the success of winning the Manjimup Bluegrass Song Lyric competition in 2016, Jenny decided there and then to try her hand at anything connected to writing to enhance her skills as a writer. And it certainly seems to have paid off.

Known for having what Jenny herself describes as a 'warped sense of humour', Jenny's pieces of writing have amused many of her fellow writers at Gosnells Writers Circle for several years. She loves nothing more than creating funny, saucy or zany cards and unique books for family and friends, especially enjoying the creative graphic design aspect.

An avid writing-competition entrant, and now long-listed three times in the Australian Writers' Centre's Furious Fiction competition, Jenny has been overheard saying, 'I am going to win this one day... just watch this space!'

A breast cancer survivor, Jenny self-publishes young children's rhymed picture books to fundraise for breast cancer research and, to date, has donated many thousands of dollars of profit to the cause. Jenny admits she produces her children's books back-to-front, meaning she starts by finding good quality clipart first; dreams up a basic storyline in her head; creates her picture pages next, and lastly, she goes back to page one and starts writing her rhymed story. Her children's books, found on www.pinkribbonbooks.org, have been sold, not only Australia-wide but world-wide. Jenny hopes that by the time today's young readers grow to adulthood, a cure for breast cancer will have been found.

Jenny Lynch lives in Perth, Western Australia,

and apparently—if book orders are anything to go by—in the hearts of children all around the globe.

https://www.pinkribbonbooks.org

https://www.facebook.com/jlynchperth

Printed in Australia
AUHW020835231222
372923AU00043B/220

9 780645 437003